Yet The Sky Is Blue

それでも空は青い

本田 つよし

Yet The Sky Is Blue

Preface

On 3 August 1945, my father left Hiroshima for evacuation to Kumamoto, his parent's homeland. Then he was a high-school student and left alone in Hiroshima by his parents because of his attendance to school. He said that something inside him had told him to run away and on the day he arrived at the destination, "death fell from the sky" in Hiroshima as the ex-president Obama described in his historical speech.

My father lost the precious things in his life——his house, his friends, and his dream of entering university. This experience made my father an atheist. He became to have no faith in any religion which could not prevent this tragedy from happening. He only believed in himself. One day he told me, "I have no regret in my life, because I have fully lived my life."

On 1 December 2019, he passed away. I cannot tell the meaning of his life, but all I can tell is that if he did not obey his inner voice in 1945, I would not be here in this world. In a sense, my life has been a journey to search for the meaning of my life.

Since my father was on the verge of death, I have become to read Buddhist books in English as much as possible. I might expect that some answer would be surely given to me through the teachings of Buddhism. One day, in a book entitled "no death, no fear" I learned that I am made of my parents, put another way, I am a continuation of my father. This realization really eases my mind even after my father's departure. His element is alive in me and my element will be alive in my children on and on.

You may notice that some of my poems in this anthology are influenced by the teachings of the Buddha. Anyway, I wish that this work would impress you, Buddhist or non-Buddhist.

With my heartfelt gratitude to the people around my family.

HONDA Tsuyoshi

序文

1945年8月3日、私の父は広島の地を離れて、両親の故郷である熊本への疎開に向かいました。当時彼は旧制中学の学生で、学業のため一人広島に残されていたのです。父の言葉によれば、心の中で「逃げろ」と告げる声があり、目的地に到着したその日に、広島には「死が空から降ってきた」のです。まさに、オバマ元米大統領が歴史的なスピーチの中で描写したように。

父は、人生において大切な数々を失いました。住んでいた家、友達、そして大学進学の夢。この経験のおかげで、彼は無神論者になりました。この悲劇を食い止められなかった宗教が信じられなくなったのです。彼にとって信じられるものは自分しかいませんでした。ある日、私に言いました。「人生に悔いはない。俺は、充分に生きた」

2019年12月1日、父は亡くなりました。父の人生の意味が何なのか、私にはわかりません。私にわかることは、1945年のあの日、父が内なる声に従っていなかったら、私はこの世界に存在していない、ということです。ある意味、私の人生は、自分が生きていることの意味を探し続ける旅だったのです。

父の死が目前になってから、私はできるだけ多くの仏教関係の

本を読むようになりました。仏教の教えを通して、何らかの答えがきっと見つかるはずだと思っていたのです。ある日、「死もなく、怖れもなく」という題名の本を読んで、自分という存在は両親が形作っている、言い換えれば、私は父の連続体である、ということを知りました。この悟りが、父が旅立った後も私の心を楽にしてくれています。

父は私の中で生き続け、そして私は私の子どもたちの中でずっと生き続けるのです。

この詩集の中の詩のいくつかが、仏教の影響下にあることに気づかれる方もいるかもしれません。何にせよ、この詩集が、仏教徒でもそうでなくても、あなたの心に残るものになることを願っています。

私の家族を取り巻く人びとへの心からの感謝を込めて。

　　　　　　　　　　　　　　　　　　　　　　本田つよし

To My Sons

私の息子たちへ

Contents

One Hug, One Help

わたしはあなたを癒せない
あなたの悲しみを消す
魔法の呪文も
あなたの痛みを取り除く
薬を手に入れる方法も
わたしにはわからない

わたしにできることは
その悲しみや痛みが
あなた自身の力で
ゆっくりと
ちょうど氷が溶けていくように
やわらいでいくのを
ほんの少し手助けするために
あなたをこの手で
そっと抱きしめられる
その日を待つ
ただそれだけなのです

I am not the one who can heal you.

I don't know

The magic word to wipe out your sorrow and

How to get the medicine to take out your pain

From your heart.

I am not the one.

All I can do is just to wait for the day

When I could embrace you in my arms

In order to warm you,

To give you one hug, one help

For making the sorrow and pain melt slowly

By themselves

Like ice cubes.

Yet The Sky Is Blue

真っ青な空の下

九十二名の命を乗せたまま
目の前の超高層ビルへと
旅客機の操縦桿を切っていく人間がいる

真っ青な空の下

爆発の恐怖から逃れようとして
その高さ二百メートルのビルの窓から
飛び降りていく人間がいる

真っ青な空の下

荒れ狂う炎を静めようとして
崩壊寸前のビルの中へと
乗り込んでいく人間がいる

真っ青な空の下

Under a pure blue sky

You see the people
Crashing a passenger plane
Into a skyscraper ahead
With 92 lives on board.

Under a pure blue sky

You see the people
Jumping out of the 200 meter-high
Windows fearful of explosion.

Under a pure blue sky

You see the people
Entering the collapsing building
To fight the raging flames.

Under a pure blue sky

人間たちが死んでいく
地上の光が届かない
真っ黒な闇へと呑み込まれていく

一人
十人
百人
何千人？

真っ青な空の下
人間たちが死んでいく

昨日までの世界が
すべて変わってしまった日
空の青さだけが
変わらない

You see the people dying

Engulfed in the deep darkness

Far from the daylight.

One,

Ten,

Hundred,

Thousands ?

Under a pure blue sky

You see the people dying.

This is the day completely changed

From the yester-world

Except from the pure blue of sky.

The Morning

終わりのない夜はない
永遠に続く闇はない

闇を深くさせるのは
人間の心だけ

朝は来る

光はきっと
あなたを照らす

There is no night that never ends.
No darkness that will be everlasting.

Only human mind can make
The darkness deeper.

The morning shall come.

The light shall certainly come
Illuminating you.

Grown-up

大人とは
待つことができる人

待つ時の重さに
静かに耐えることができる人

そして
その待つ人が
自分の運命を変えるかもしれない
重要な人だったとしても

大人なら

きっと静かに待っている

A grown-up is the person
Who can wait.

The person who can quietly endure
The burden of waiting time.

And
Even if the one he is waiting for
Might be the important presence
That changes his fortune.

He as a grown-up must be
Quietly waiting.

20th Century

二十世紀とは
理性と残虐性の時代だった

研ぎ澄まされた理性が技術を生み
計測可能な幸福をもたらした

追い詰められた理性が
狂気へと反転して
計り知れぬ不幸をもたらした

　二十世紀に生まれた僕たちは
幸福なのか不幸なのか

その答えが出せるのは
二十一世紀に生まれた
君たちだけなのかもしれない

The 20th century was
The age of reason and cruelty.

Sharpened reason produced technologies
That brought measurable happiness.

Driven reason turn into insanity
That brought unmeasurable unhappiness.

Whether are we, born in the 20th century,
Happy or unhappy ?

The answer might only be
In the hands of you
Who are born in the 21st century.

The Sandman

不意に
ウトウトしてはいけない
世界から離れていく
その一瞬の間際に
悪魔が耳元で
ささやくから

Never feel sleepy

Unexpectedly.

At the moment of falling in another world,

The demon will

Whisper

Into your ear.

Understanding

今　考えて
どうしてもわからないことは
いっそ考えないほうが良い

いつの日か
わかる時が来る

たとえば
死ぬ間際の
一瞬の時に

You had better give up thinking

About the matter that you never understand

Now.

Someday

You will understand that.

Someday

Such as the moment

You die.

Don't Think Twice

考えすぎるな

考えすぎると
足は止まり
舌は鈍り
耳はふさがれて
遊び心をなくしていく

考えすぎるな

Don't think twice.

Thinking too much
Makes you stop,
Dulls your tongue,
Blocks your ears,
And ruins your playful mind.

Don't Think Twice.

Black-bird

暗闇で迷わず
飛び続ける鳥になれ

信じる方へ
飛び続ければ

たとえ
地上の人々すべてを照らす
太陽にはなれなくても

いつかきっと
誰かの道しるべとして
頭上に輝く
星になれるから

Be a bird flying on

Without losing your direction

In the darkness.

Keeping the direction you believe

Will surely make you a star

That shines as a signpost for

Somebody, someday,

Even though not becoming the sun

Illuminating all the people

On this planet.

Spillover

身体の中に貯め込んだ

言葉が
　　　　音楽が
　　　　　　　映像が

ついに漏れ出したから
もう後には戻れない

After staying stocked in my body,

The words,

       The music,

             The images

Have finally spilled over,

I can no longer get back.

HANA-BI

11月1日
午前5時55分
目が覚める

頭の中では
HANA-BI が
鳴っている

Date 11.1

5:55 a.m.

I woke up.

The sound of HANA-BI

Is lingering

In my brain.

Destiny

運命を決めるのは
神殿の壁に書かれた言葉ではなく
預言者の口から出るお告げでもない

運命を決めるのは
一瞬交す視線と視線
そして
指と指が触れた時に走る
あの電流だ

A destiny should be decided
Not by the words written on the wall,
Neither by the oracle of a prophet.

A destiny should be decided
By those instant glances
Among two people,
And by the electric touch
Between their fingers.

Salvation

私はあなたを救えない
そうではなく
あなたは救われるようにできている
普通にしていれば
普通に救われるし
ややこしくしていれば
救われるのもややこしくなるけれど
必ず最後に救われる

私はあなたを救えない
そうではなく
あなた自身が
初めから救われるようにできている

I cannot save you.

The truth is that

You are made to be saved.

If you live a normal life,

You will be saved normally.

If you live a complicated life,

You will be saved at the last day

Even though in a complicated way.

I cannot save you.

The truth is that

You yourself are made to be saved

From the very beginning.

Mission

あなたが、あなたであること
それが、あなたの使命
私が、私であること
それが、私の使命

簡単なようで、むずかしい
むずかしいようで、簡単

なぜなら、そもそも、
宇宙は、そんな使命たちで
できているから

To be who you are,

That's your mission.

To be who I am,

That's my mission.

It seems easy, but it's difficult.

It seems difficult, but it's easy.

Because, from the beginning,

The universe is made of

Such missions.

Your compassion is not for others
（情けは人のためならず）

愛は痛みをともなう
思いやりは癒しをもたらす
愛は時に人を殺し
思いやりが人を殺すことはない

他人への思いやりはめぐりめぐって
いつか自分自身を救うのだ

思いやり、慈悲、情けは
他人のためだけでなく
自分のためにもある

Love hurts.

Compassion heals.

Love sometimes kills.

Compassion never kills.

Compassion for others will

Save yourself in return someday.

Your compassion is not only for others,

But also for yourself.

Love‐Craving = Compassion

愛が世界を救う、と誰かが言う
でも愛はすべてを受けいれすぎて
人間の暗黒面をも受け入れる
だから、愛から渇愛を取り除こう

愛−渇愛＝慈悲
慈悲は、欲しがらない愛
慈悲は、与える愛

これらの方程式で世界を救える

Some say love saves the world.

But love is so much inclusive

And can include even the dark side of man.

So I say we should take away craving from love.

Love − Craving = Compassion

Compassion = Love without craving

Compassion = Love for giving

These equations can save the world.

Amida

アミダとは思いやりの化身
アミダとは人間の本性
アミダとは私たち自身
ありがたや　ありがたや
ナムアミダブツ

Amida is the embodiment of compassion.

Amida is the true human nature.

Amida is ourselves.

How grateful I feel.

Namu Amida Butsu.

Religion

物事が上手く行っているとき
たいていの人は宗教を必要としない
けれども、
どうしようもない状況に直面したら
そのとき初めて
人は宗教に出会う
まるで恋の出会いのように
私にとって宗教は
知識を超えたもの
それは、まさに、経験だ

When things are going smoothly,

Most people don't need any religion.

But once you face

A desperate situation,

You will encounter a religion

For the first time,

Like a boy meets a girl.

For me,

Religion is beyond knowledge.

It is definitely an experience.

One

すべてのものには
ひとつにしようとする力が
働いており
人はこれを「神」とよぶ

すべてのものは
ひとつになろうとする力を
持っており
人はこれを「愛」と呼ぶ

On everything

There is a power

To make it one.

People call this "God."

Within everything

There is a power

To become one.

People call this "love."

God

「神」とは存在そのもの
すべてのものを抱きしめ
すべての人を救う
果てしない力

だから、不完全な人間のように
どこか外側に「いる」のではなく
神は、ここ内側に「ある」のだ

"God" is Being itself.
That embraces everything
And saves everyone.
It is an infinite power.

So not as imperfect human,
It does not "live" there outside.
God "is" here inside.

Life

見えていても見えていなくても
あなたの目の前に
人生はちゃんとある

あなたのほうから逃げない限り
人生は決して逃げたりしないで
そこにある

だから
おいしい人生が逃げてしまう
などとあせったりしないで
ひとつしかない人生と
まっすぐに向き合って
自分にできることを
毎日ちゃんと続けていけば
それでいいのだ

Your life is there

In front of you,

No matter how you can see it.

Your life never run away from you

As long as you do not run away.

Your life is there.

So

Face your life straightforward

Not being panicked by worry of

Your "delicious" life running away.

Keep doing what you can do everyday.

That is the way.

The Selected Person

選ばれた人とは
人より
物事がスムーズに行く人ではなく
人より
多くの困難を背負った人

選ばれた人とは
多くの困難に立ち向かうことで
その人らしさを磨き上げてゆく

その困難を乗り越えることで
より人としての「完璧」に
近づいてゆく

思いもかけなかった
困難に出会った時
人は言う「なぜ私に？」

それはあなたが
選ばれた人だからです

The selected person is
Not the one who goes more smoothly
Than others do,
But the one who has more difficulties
Than others do.

The selected person will hone up
His or her personality
By facing difficulties.

Overcoming the difficulties
Will bring him or her closer
To "perfection" as human being.

When you come across
An unexpected difficulty,
You will say, "Why me?"

I say
"Because you are the selected person."

Real Love

あなたに出会って初めて
人にやさしくすることは
自分に厳しくすることだと知った

あなたに出会って初めて
人を愛することと
自分を愛することの間にある
近くて遠い距離を知った

あなたに出会って初めて
心が熱くなればなるほど
頭を冷やすことが大切だと知った

今
ぼくは誰よりも
あなたに熱く焦がれ
誰よりも冷静に
これからの道を探している

それこそが

I never knew the truth
That being gentle to others means
Being strict to myself
Until I met you.

I never knew the distance
That could be either close or far
Between loving someone and
Loving myself
Until I met you.

I never knew the importance of
Cooling down my brain,
The more I am heating up my heart
Until I met you.

Now
I am searching for the coolest way
With the hottest heart toward you
Than anybody.

今
ぼくにできる精一杯の
Real Love

That is my wholehearted way of

Real Love for you

At the present moment.

No Alternative Love

誰かを欲望の代わりにすることは
ぎりぎり許されたとしても
誰かを愛の代わりにすることは
けっして許されない

それは
ほんとうに愛する相手を
裏切るだけでなく
自分自身の気持ちを
いちばん裏切ることだから

強く
時には痛いほどの愛から目をそらして
その代わりに
甘く
やさしいだけの愛を求め続けると
最後には
誰を愛すればいいのか
わからなくなるから

You are barely forgiven to have someone

For your alternative desire.

You are never ever forgiven to have someone

For your alternative love.

Because that's not only the way to betray

Your true lover,

But also the way to betray

Your true heart the most.

You are avoiding the strong and

Sometimes hurting love.

Instead you are craving for

The love that is just sweet and soft.

You will not be able to tell

Who to love

At the end.

Sleepless Night

眠れない夜
身体と心が裂けていく

泥沼のように疲れた身体の底で
地上のあなたを求めて
心の泡が
浮かび上がろうとして

眠れない夜
絶望と希望をいっしょに抱えながら
スローモーションで
鉛色のまどろみへと
落ちていく
　　　　落ちていく
　　　　　　落ちていく

My body is torn apart from my mind
At sleepless night.

Exhausted like muddy water
My mind is struggling for you above
Just like a bubble is going up from
The muddy water.

Holding despair and hope together
I am falling into a leaden slumber
In slow-motion.
Falling,
            Falling,
                        Falling,
                                    At sleepless night.

Gap

愛　それは
ギャップを埋めたいという
気持ち

ギャップのあるところ
どこでも
愛の磁力が働いている

愛　それは
ギャップを埋めて
ひとつをめざす
甘く
時には狂おしいまでの
引力

そして
埋まるはずのないギャップが
埋められたと
錯覚した時
最初にかけられた

Love is wanting
To fill a gap.

Wherever there is a gap,
Magnetic force of love works.

Love is the force of gravity
That is sweet and sometimes crazy
To fill a gap and unite two.

And
When you have an illusion of
Having the gap filled
That could be impossible,
The spell of love cast on you is gone
With no reason.

Love is a karma
That sadly keeps searching for
A gap.

愛の魔法は
なぜか
消えてしまう

愛　それは
悲しくなるほど
ギャップを探し続けてしまう
人間の業

Fun

好きな音楽を聴いている時
耳が楽しい

好きな物を食べている時
舌が楽しい

好きな風景を見ている時
目が楽しい

そして
好きな人と一緒にいる時
魂が楽しい

When you listen to your loved music,

Your ears have fun.

When you eat your loved food,

Your tongue has fun.

When you see your loved scenery,

Your eyes have fun.

And

When you stay with your loved one,

Your soul has fun.

The Woman

なくしたものを探して
見つからず
フラフラ歩いて
たどりついたところで
顔をあげたら
目の前に
その人は
立っていた

なぜ　なくしたのか
今になって気がついた

その人に
出会うためだったと

When I was walking dizzy,
Never found the lost,
I reached the place where
I held my head up
And saw the woman
Standing in front of me.

Now I know the reason
Why I lost.

To meet that woman.

Science

科学の最大の罪は
人間をラクにするという
その効能だけに
人間の心を傾かせてしまったことだ

人間
ラクばかりしていると
ロクなことはない

The greatest sin of science lies

In a tendency of man

Who prefers to be easy

Because of its effectiveness.

You know.

Easy come,

Easy go.

Life Needs 4Cs
（人生は 4C）

人生は
勇気と
礼儀と
ユーモア
そして
少しのお金があれば
だいじょうぶ

愛は必要ないのか　だって？
あれは
良くわからないが
生きている限り
イヤでも
ついてくるものだ

Life goes well

If you have

Courage,

Courtesy,

Common Sense of Humor and

A little Cash.

No need for Love?

Don't worry.

Love follows you

Wherever you go,

However you like it or not.

A Flower Of Your Heart

ひがむな
うらむな
心が腐る

ただただ感謝し
感謝されれば
やがて
心の花が咲く

Have no unfair feeling.

Have no grudge.

If not, your heart will decay.

Just keep thanking,

And being thanked.

Before long,

A flower of your heart will bloom.

With Your Whole Heart
（まごころをこめて）

親がわが子に
教えられることは
知識でも
道徳でも
信仰でもなく

「まごころをこめて」
何かをするということだ

それは言葉ではなく
親その人の生き方
つまり行動でしか伝わらない

書物やネットからではなく
親というモデルに接することで
子どもは、「まごころをこめて」
何かをすることの大切さを
学ぶと思うのです

What a parent can teach

His or her child is,

Not knowledge,

Not morality,

Not faith,

But to do something

"With his or her whole heart."

That should not be conveyed

By a parent's words,

But only by his or her way of life

That is action.

Not from books or Internet,

But from facing the parent

As a role-model,

The child can learn

The importance of doing something

"With his or her whole heart."

Love ?

愛とは何か？
正直に言って
良くわからないのです

でも
今
目の前にいる人が
自分にとって
一番大切な人だ
ということだけは
良くわかっています

What is love?

Honestly saying,

I have no idea.

But

Now I have a confidence

That the woman

In front of me is

The most precious presence

For me.

A Will

何も信じない
何も疑わない
ただ
あるがままを
感謝して受け入れ
その時その時を
前向きに楽しめば
それでいい

I believe nothing.

I doubt nothing.

I just accept things as they are

With gratitude and

Enjoy every moment of my life

Positively.

That's all.

The Overdose Of Love

過剰な愛は人をダメにする
なぜなら　人は誰かを
四六時中愛することなどできないから

だから覚えておいて
つねに生きることが先決だと

愛の過剰摂取にご用心
ちゃんと生きて　そして愛そう

Too much love would spoil you

Because you cannot love someone

24 hours that is true.

So remember,

Always life comes first.

Beware the overdose of love.

Be in love while you really live.

Precious

大切なものほど
自分の手で
なくしてしまう
それが人間
人間の心の弱さ
なぜなら
本当に大切なものほど
自分の存在そのものを
脅かしてしまうから

持ち続けるのが怖いほど
大切なもの
それは時に
「愛」と呼ばれている

郵 便 は が き

112-8790

105

東京都文京区関口1-23-6
東洋出版 編集部 行

||||·|||·||·|·|·||·|||·|·|||·|·|||·||·|·||·||·|·|·|||·||·||·||||

本のご注文はこのはがきをご利用ください

●ご注文の本は、小社が委託する本の宅配会社ブックサービス㈱より、1週間前後でお届けいたします。代金は、お届けの際、下記金額をお支払いください。

お支払い金額＝税込価格＋手数料305円

●電話やFAXでもご注文を承ります。
電話 03-5261-1004　　FAX 03-5261-1002

ご注文の書名	税込価格	冊　数

● 本のお届け先　※下記のご連絡先と異なる場合にご記入ください。

ふりがな お名前	お電話番号
ご住所　〒　　　　－	

e-mail　　　　　　　　　　　　＠

東洋出版の書籍をご購入いただき、誠にありがとうございます。
今後の出版活動の参考とさせていただきますので、アンケートにご協力
いただきますよう、お願い申し上げます。

● この本の書名

....

● この本は、何でお知りになりましたか?(複数回答可)
　1. 書店　2. 新聞広告(　　　　　　新聞)　3. 書評・記事　4. 人の紹介
　5. 図書室・図書館　6. ウェブ・SNS　7. その他(　　　　　　　　　　)

....

● この本をご購入いただいた理由は何ですか?(複数回答可)
　1. テーマ・タイトル　2. 著者　3. 装丁　4. 広告・書評
　5. その他(　　　　　　　　　　　　　　　　　　　　　　)

....

● 本書をお読みになったご感想をお書きください

....

● 今後読んでみたい書籍のテーマ・分野などありましたらお書きください

....

ご感想を匿名で書籍のPR等に使用させていただくことがございます。
ご了承いただけない場合は、右の□内に✓をご記入ください。　　□許可しない

※メッセージは、著者にお届けいたします。差し支えない範囲で下欄もご記入ください。

● ご職業　1.会社員　2.経営者　3.公務員　4.教育関係者　5.自営業　6.主婦
　　　　　 7.学生　8.アルバイト　9.その他(　　　　　　　　　　　　)

● お住まいの地域

　　　　都道府県　　　　　　　　市町村区　男・女　年齢　　　　歳

ご協力ありがとうございました。

The more precious a thing is
The more likely you can lose it
By yourself.
That's the way you are.
That's the way your vulnerable mind is,
Because the more precious a thing is
The more likely it threatens you and
Your presence.

When you feel scared of holding it long
Because it is too precious to hold,
You sometimes call it
"LOVE".

No Romance

運命の人を信じない
愛の言葉を信じない
永遠の誓いを信じない

ただ　今　ここで
生きて通い合う
気持ちと気持ちだけを
しっかりと
抱きしめていたい

たとえ　それが
すくってもすくっても
掌からこぼれ落ちていく
砂のように
時間とともに
消え去っていくものだと
わかっていても

I don't believe a woman of fate.

I don't believe a word of love.

I don't believe an eternal promise.

I just want to tightly hold these feelings

That come and go between us

Vividly here and now.

Even if I know that those feelings are

Vanishing second by second

Just like grains of sand

Spilling over

Out of my palms

No matter how I try to scoop them back.

Demon

仏^{ほとけ}心^{ごころ}は生^{なま}殺^{ごろ}し

ならば鬼^きとなり悪^{あく}となり

一気に殺してくださいな

With Buddha mind,

You are killing and rescuing me.

So please kill me instantly

With Demon mind.

Preparation
（覚悟）

毅然としなさい
ナイーブにならず

大人になりなさい
子どもっぽいのはダメ

もう無邪気ではいられない
だって残り少ない人生だから

肝に銘じなさい
日々、死へと近づいていることを

Be ruthless.
Don't be naive.

Be mature.
Don't be childish.

You can't be innocent anymore,
'Cause your days are already numbered.

You should know
You're going to die day by day.

Thanks

ただ歩けることの
ありがたさは
一歩も歩けなくなった後に
初めてわかる

ただ食べられることの
ありがたさは
一口も食べられなくなった後に
初めてわかる

ただ考えられることの
ありがたさは
何も考えられなくなった後に
初めてわかる

ありがとう
ありがとう
ただ生きている
そのことに
心の底から

You realize that just walking is

A miracle

When you end up

Not being able to take one step.

You realize that just eating is

A miracle

When you end up

Not being able to have one bite.

You realize that just thinking is

A miracle

When you end up

Not being able to have one idea.

Thousand thanks for

Just being alive.

I am so grateful for it

From the bottom of my heart.

ありがとう

Good-by
（サヨナラ）

出会いは
サヨナラのはじまり

どんな出会いも
その先には
サヨナラが待っている

サヨナラ　サヨナラ

別れはすべてつらいけれど
人はサヨナラを言うたびに
気持ちが引き締まり
少しずつ強くなっていく

サヨナラを怖れているあいだは
出会いも
やって来ない

サヨナラは
出会いのはじまり

To meet someone is
A beginning of saying good-by.

Any encounter awaits
Saying good-by
After that.

Good-by and good-by.

Every separation has pain
But every time you say good-by
You brace yourself up and
Get stronger little by little.

While you are afraid of
Saying good-by,
No encounter will come to you.

Saying good-by is
A beginning of meeting someone.

Avoid Negative Speakers

ネガティブさん
ネガティブさん
おひきとりください

Mr. Negative

Mr. Negative

Will you please leave me alone ?

Grown-up

大人とは
しがみつかない人
大人とは
そっと抱きしめる人

No grown-up

Will cling onto you.

A grown-up

Will hold you softly.

Deep Water

湖のような人になりたい

河のような人になりたい

海のような人になりたい

I want to be like a lake,

Like a great river,

And like the ocean.

Life

一度失ったものは
二度と取り返すことができない
それが人生

その気になれば
何度でも
やり直すことができる
それも人生

Once you lose something,

You can never take it back.

That's the way a life is.

As long as you have a will,

You can restart your life

Again and again.

That's the way it is, too.

The Presence Of Manuel Legris

それは
天に向かって
まっすぐに伸びてゆく
一本の樹

それは
見上げる人すべてを包み込む
大きな木陰

それは
天から与えられたものを
真に生かしている人に
出会えた時の
奇跡のような
しあわせ

Like a tree reaching for the heaven,

Like a shade giving all the people the haven,

With his turning a God's gift into a presence,

Seeing him is miraculous happiness.

Person With An Inner Star

心に星を持つ人は
たとえ暗闇の中にいても
どこか輝いている

心に星を持つ人が
その星について話し出すと
たちまち瞳の奥から
光があふれ始める

心に星を持つ人の回りには
道を見失った人々が
自然に集まって来る

心に星を持つ人は
自分がどこから来て
どこへ行こうとしているのか
知っている

A person with an inner star
Will shine somehow
Even in the darkness.

When the person with an inner star
Begins to talk about the star within,
Hidden light will immediately flow
Out of the eyes.

Lost people will gather
Around the person with an inner star
Spontaneously.

The person with an inner star knows
Where he or she comes from and
Where to go.

Chagall
（シャガール）

その赤は生きるために

その青は羽ばたくために

The Red is there to live.

The Blue is there to fly.

Words

朝
人を元気づけた言葉が
夜になると
人を落ち込ませる

夜
人を安心させた言葉が
朝になると
不安の種に変わる

しあわせへと昇っていく
光輝く階段にも
ふしあわせへと沈んでいく
暗い落とし穴にもなる
この
言葉という
必要悪を
とにもかくにも
人間は
身につけてしまったのだ

The words that cheer you up

In the morning

Let you down

At night.

The words that make you feel safe

At night

Turn into a seed of anxiety

Next morning.

The words that can be

An illuminating stairway to happiness or

Can be a dark pitfall down to unhappiness,

Have we gotten in anyway,

Even if they are an necessary evil.

If we don't want to get back to being animals

In the first place,

We have to get along well with

This double-edged sword.

今さら
ケダモノに戻りたくなければ
この両刃の剣と
上手くつきあっていくしかない

Words II

どんな時でも
なにか言葉がないと
安心できない
という癖がある人間は
いつまでたっても
ふしあわせのままだ

たとえ
いつまでも消えない言葉として
カタチに残すことはできなくても
静寂を
沈黙を
抱きしめられる人だけが
次々と消えていく
一秒一秒を
しあわせな瞬間に
変えていくことができる

If you have a habit of

Not feeling secured

Without any words

Any time,

You can never ever be happy.

If you have capacity of embracing

Stillness, silence,

Even if you cannot preserve it

As the words that will never vanish,

You will only be able to turn

Every second that is vanishing

Into a happy moment.

Negative

せっかく
前向きな気持ちに
してくれる人なのに
何か言わなくては
という焦りが
後ろ向きな言葉を
言わせてしまう

その
みずから仕掛けた罠に
いつまでも
はまったまま
ただオロオロと
うろたえているうちに

言われた
その人が
くるりと踵を返して
後ろを向き
やがて顔が

Since she makes me feel positive,

I have to say something as long as I can.

The impatience urges me to say

Negative words to her.

While I am bound in this trap I have created,

Panicky for ever and ever,

She turns her back on me

And is going,

Going,

Going,

Gone.

見えなくなる
見えなく
なる
見えなく
な
る

It's Nice To Be Myself
（わたしで、よかった）

日本人じゃなきゃ
よかったのに
この家族に
生まれてこなけりゃ
よかったのに

もし　そんな思いを
胸にくすぶらせたまま
暮らしているとしたら
どんどん　どんどん
暗いほうへ　暗いほうへ
歩いていってしまうよ
まるで
ブラックホールに
吸いこまれていくように

人は
自分が自分であることの
ありがたさを
ゆっくりと噛みしめ

I wish I were not
A Japanese...
I wish I had not been
Born in this family...

If those feelings dwells
In your mind,
Your life will be approaching
To darker and darker place,
As though being vacuumed
Into Black Hole.

I think you will never step forward
Until you savor and thank for
The presence of yourself
Then make it nourish you.

Just let the people label you
Say, right-wing or anachronism.
Those are who try to force individuals

それを栄養にすることで
前へ進んでいけると
思うのだ

右翼だとか
時代錯誤だとか
ひとりひとりの事情もわからずに
何か大きなカッコで
人間をひとくくりにしようとする人には
言わせておけばいいじゃないか

あの
川にうつった
自分を見て
ほっとした
くまさんのように
わたしで
よかった
わたしが
わたしで

Into big brackets

Without understanding each situation.

Just like the bear who got relief

Watching his own reflection on the river,

Let's restart your life with thinking this way

"It's nice to be myself.

It's really nice to be nobody but me.

Thanks a thousand times!"

ほんとうによかった

ありがたい

ありがとう

そう思うことから
はじめてみようよ

Open Sesame

開けてください
開けてください

開けゴマ
開けゴマ

確かに言葉は
扉の向こう側にいる
その人に
気持ちを伝えているのかもしれない

でも
歌を歌うのはどうだろう
もしオンチだったら
楽器を演奏するのはどうだろう
それもできなければ
自己流でいいから
タップダンスをドタドタ鳴らすのは
どうだろう
そのほうがもっと

Please open the door.
Please open the door.

Open Sesame.
Open Sesame.

Those words might convey
Your feeling to the one
Behind the door
For sure.

But
Why don't you sing a song?
If you are a terrible singer,
Why don't you play some instrument?
If you are not good at it,
Why don't you tap-dance loudly
Even if it is in your own style.
Those actions would convey
Your feeling more.

気持ちが伝わるかもしれない

そして
自分の手で
ノブを回し
そっと扉を押してみたら
どうだろう

もしかしたら
鍵はもう
開いているかもしれないのだ

Then

Why don't you turn the knob and

Push the door gently?

The door might already be

OPEN !

Real Love

いちばん大切な人なのに
いちばん酷_{ひど}いことを
してしまうかもしれない
それが Real Love

いちばん好きな人なのに
いちばん嫌われるかもしれない
それが Real Love

そして
いちばん憶病になってしまいそうな時に
いちばん勇気を出さなければならない
それが
Real Love

You might do the most cruel thing

Even to the most precious one.

That's Real Love.

You might be hated most

Even by the most loved one.

That's Real Love.

And

You have to get the No.1 courage

Even when you are likely to have

No.1 cowardice.

That's Real Love.

Growing-up

人は悲しみとともに
大人になる
言い換えれば
悲しみを知らない人間は
けっして大人になれないのだ

A man will grow up

With a certain sorrow.

In other words,

A man who never knows sorrow

Will never ever grow up.

You're the one who can make it

ちょっと冷たい言い方かも
知れませんが
あなたを幸せにできるのは
あなたしかいません

お父さんでも
お母さんでもなく
お兄さんでも
お姉さんでもなく
弟や妹でもない
恋人や夫や妻や
そして我が子でもなく
もちろん上司でも部下でもない
そして人によっては
神様でも仏様でもなく
自分を幸せにできるのは
自分しかいない

そう覚悟を決めた時から
あなたは確実に

It may be a little bit indifferent saying,

But it is sure that you are the only person

Who can make you happy.

Not your father,

Not your mother,

Not your big brother,

Not your big sister,

Not your younger brother and sister,

Not your lover and spouse,

Not your child,

Not your boss and staff, of course,

And for some people

Not God and Buddha but you are

The only being that makes you happy.

Just from when you realize

And determine to accept this,

You can step forward

To happiness for sure.

幸せに向かって
一歩踏み出している
と思うのです

You are so beautiful to me

ある朝のこと
開店したばかりの
小さなオープンカフェの前を通りながら
ふと思った

一度も言葉を交わしたことがない
そのウェイトレスが
ただひたすら
真っ白なテーブルを
もっとピカピカにしようと
クロスで拭いている

男の子みんなが振り向くほどの
美人ではなく
どこにでもいるような女の子だけれど
今はただ一心に
誰の視線を気にすることもなく
テーブルを拭いている
その姿を見て
ふと思った

One morning
I happened to think
While passing in front of
A small open-air café.

The waitress who I'd never
Talked with before,
Was wiping a pure-white table
Single-mindedly
To make it shine more.

She is not the pretty one who
Every boy will look back at,
But is just like the girl next door.
I happened to think,
Seeing her cleaning the table
Single-mindedly.

I will face my loved one
As honestly as possible

どんなにイヤなことがあっても
僕にとって大切な人には
できる限り誠実に
そして
たとえ僕を苦しめる人にも
人としての礼儀を忘れずに
とにかくズルをしないで
僕もちゃんと
働いていこう

When anything happened to me.

And

I will also do my job

As earnestly as possible

With courtesy and sincerity

Even to the one who suffers me.

Bad thing happens because of me
Good thing happens because of you
（悪いことは自分のせい
　良いことはあなたのおかげ）

私が行動を起こさない限り

何も起こらない

あなたが行動を起こさない限り

何も起こらない

つまり

人生において

ひとりでに起きることなど

何ひとつなく

我々が常に起こしているのだ

だから、私の心構えはこうなる

悪いことは自分のせいだから

謙虚に次は良くするよう努め

良いことはあなたのおかげだから

Nothing will happen
Until I take action.
Nothing will happen
Until you take action.

In a word
There's nothing
That happens by itself to us in our life.
That means
We always MAKE it happen.

So I have this attitude of mind as follows.

Since I made the bad thing happen
I should be modest and try to get it better
Next time.

いつも感謝の気持ちを忘れない

Since you made the good thing happen

I should be grateful to you

All the time.

101-steps-away-happiness
（101 歩目のしあわせ）

10 歩あるいても
しあわせになれなかった

50 歩あるいても
しあわせになれなかった

そして 100 歩あるいてみて
ほとんどの人は
「やっぱり
しあわせにはなれないんだ」
と独り言のようにつぶやいて
とぼとぼと引き返していく
でも
ほんとうは
あと 1 歩踏み出していたら
まるで
同じ道を 100 歩
歩き続けた者にだけ
そっと与えられる
ご褒美のように

You took 10 steps forward
Not to find happiness.

You took 50 steps forward
Not to find happiness.

And most of people took
100 steps forward to say by themselves
" I knew I could not find happiness
After all."
Plodding back to the place
Where they came.

But to tell the truth,
One more step would make you
Find some presence standing there,
As if a small reward for your keeping
100 steps in one direction.

It would stand there

そこに立っているものに
気がついたかもしれない

何気ない顔をして
昔からの友だちのように
そこに立っている
101 歩目のしあわせに
気がついたかもしれない
だから
あと 1 歩！
前へ！

With an innocent face

As if it were an old friend of you

Waiting to be found.

So take one more step forward

To meet

The 101-steps-away-happeness !

Nobody can serve happiness to you

おいしい料理を銀の皿に載せて
あなたに提供することはできる
楽しい時間も金のゲートがある
どこかの場所で提供することができる
でも、たとえどこにいようと
あなたにしあわせを提供することは
けっして　けっして　できない

だから本当にしあわせが欲しければ
他の誰でもなく
あなただけが
あなた自身にしあわせを提供できる
ということに気がつきなさい

A delicious meal can be served to you
On a silver plate.
An amusing time can be served to you
Where there are some golden gates.
But you can never ever
Be served happiness
Nowhere you were.

So if you really want it true
You should know that
Nobody can serve happiness to you,
Nobody but you
Can do that.

Dream

夢は
何のためにあるのか？

夢は
かなえるためにある

夢は
誰かの心に
生まれた瞬間から
かなえられたくて
かなえられたくて
ウズウズしながら
待っている

それは
花のつぼみが
咲きたくて
咲きたくて
その日を
待ち続けているのに

What is a dream there for ?

A dream is there for
Coming true.

A dream has been itching and waiting
Badly to come true
Since it was born in
Somebody's mind.

It's just like a bud of flower
That has kept waiting badly
For the day to bloom.

So, a dream is there for
Coming true.

とても良く似ている

だから
夢は
かなえるために
あるのです

Between Like And Love

だから好き、は
Like に近づき
だけど好き、は
Love に近づく

思い合う
二人の気持ちは
いつも
このふたつのあいだを
揺れている

"So, I 'm into you."

Sounds you like someone.

"But, I'm into you."

Sounds you love someone.

The hearts of two people

Who are attracted to each other,

Always sway

Between Like and Love.

I Wish

要は男性がどれだけ真剣に
女性の幸せと美しさを願っているかだ

もし男性が女性を
自分の幸せのために
利用しようとしたら
その瞬間にすべては崩れる

だから私は心から願うのだ
君よ
いつまでも
幸せに、そして
美しくあれ

It depends on

How much earnest

A man wish

A woman be happy and beautiful.

If he should

Try to use her

For the sake of

His own happiness,

It must collapse

At that moment.

So I wish,

From the bottom of my heart,

You be

HAPPY AND BEAUTIFUL

FOR LIFE.

Happiness

しあわせは生モノだから
今ここにあるしあわせを
抱きしめて
噛みしめる
それしかないのだ

Happiness is something like perishables.

So all you can do is

Hold it tight and

Taste it thoroughly

Here and now.

Happiness II

幸せは決して予約できない
賢者の言葉によれば
幸せとは
今ここでしか実現しないもの
だから過去からも
未来からさえも
自由になって
今この瞬間を大切にして
今ここで
幸せになろう

You can never make a reservation

For happiness.

As wise men said

Happiness can only be possible

In the here and now.

So be free from the past

And even from the future,

Just cherish

The present moment

And be happy

Here and now.

詩とは書くものではなく生まれてくるもの。

たとえ、それが祝福された言葉だったとしても、

呪われた言葉だったとしても、

詩は自らの生命力で生まれ落ちてくる。だから、

書こうとして書いたものは、いつも詩にはならず、

ある瞬間に生まれ落ちて来るものを掌で受け止めて、

白いスペースにそっと立たせてあげれば、

それが「詩」になっている、

と思うのですが、はたして……。

本田つよし

A poem should not be written but be born.

Even if it consists of celebrated words or cursed words,

A poem is delivered down by its own power. So

I always try to write it and fail but catch it with my palms

To let it stand gently on a white space.

In such a way I think I have made *a poem*.

Haven't I ?

HONDA Tsuyoshi

HONDA Tsuyoshi
本田つよし

Profile
プロフィール

Born in Kumamoto Prefecture. Graduated from Waseda University.
熊本県生まれ。早稲田大学第一文学部英文学科卒業。

Weblog "English for Happiness"
ブログ「しあわせになる英語」
https://www.englishforhappiness.com/

Twitter
ツイッター
https://twitter.com/englishforhapp

A member of the Steering Committee of "Sangha for Studying and Practicing Buddhism Through Basic English"
「仏教を初歩英語で学び実践するサンガの会」運営委員

Yet The Sky Is Blue
それでも空は青い

発行日	2020 年 10 月 19 日　第 1 刷発行

著者	本田 つよし（ほんだ・つよし）

発行者	田辺修三
発行所	東洋出版株式会社

〒 112-0014　東京都文京区関口 1-23-6
電話　03-5261-1004（代）　振替　00110-2-175030
http://www.toyo-shuppan.com/

印刷・製本	日本ハイコム株式会社

許可なく複製転載すること、または部分的にもコピーすることを禁じます。
乱丁・落丁の場合は、ご面倒ですが、小社までご送付下さい。
送料小社負担にてお取り替えいたします。

© Tsuyoshi Honda　2020, Printed in Japan
ISBN 978-4-8096-7999-5　定価はカバーに表示してあります

ISO14001 取得工場で印刷しました